The Nuts

Alex M Wright

For Zevie and Lara

Published by AMWT Books
Text and original illustrations © copyright 2020
by Alex M Wright
All rights reserved

Two peas in a pod were Percy and Pippa.
When Pippa's not there, Percy will miss her.

See Percy was shy,
Pippa's young brother.

Whilst she'd seek adventure,
He'd run for cover.

She always urged Percy
To come out and play.

I know you'd have fun if you tried it!

She'd say.

Mummy nut said:

Don't worry my son!
Rather than frowning
Go out and have fun!

Mummy nut meant well.
A good mum she was too.
She loved them so much,
That another was due!

But she was always so busy
And Percy just knew,
Pippa'd found trouble!
What was he to do?

He'd rather stay in
Not out of his shell.
What fears lurked outside?
No nut could tell!

But Percy so loved Pip;
Oh how he missed her!
And now he was worried
For his brave big sister!

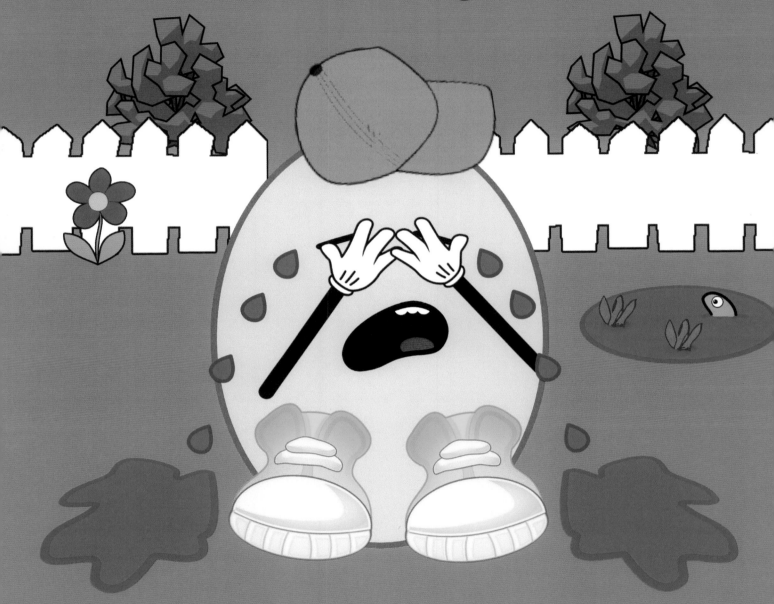

What if this time
She'd gone too far?
Strayed past the street corner?
Got trapped in a jar?

Or worse still,
Percy's heart stuttered;
She'd been squashed to a spread,
Become peanut butter!

So he took a deep breath,
Turned his frown upside-down,
Strode out of his house...

...and into Nut Town!

For this search he'd need wisdom.
This was no easy task!
He knew where to turn;
The wrinkly walnuts he'd ask!

Percy's old neighbours
Lived just down the lane.
So wrinkly and wise,
They knew just why he came!

This gang of misfits
Seem scary to me...

Thought Percy, approaching
The cool gang of three.

The mixed nuts they eyed him,
As Percy came near.
The nut knot in his stomach
Grew along with his fear.

But then they were chatting.
Percy soon felt a klutz!
They weren't at all scary,
Despite being mixed nuts!

They laughed and shared stories
And then in the end,
Percy found with surprise,
He'd become their new friend!

The Almond Sisters!
Thought the shy little nut.
They're so pretty, so perfect!
Fear churned in his gut.

And so he pressed on
And just down the street
Were the Almond Sisters,
So golden and neat.

They really were pretty,
And while Percy was scared,
The Almonds they turned to him

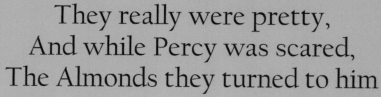

They brewed Percy some tea,
The nicest he'd had.
And he thought to himself,
Almonds really aren't bad.

They may be pretty,
Unblemished and smooth,
But they're so very friendly.
It appears I've been rude.

Not at all!

Said the Almonds

We're so pleased you came!
Your sister sent word:
'Keep playing my game!'

A game? Thought Percy,
Oh my my my no!
My sister's in trouble
And so I must go!

To the beach! Cried the sisters

She's there now, it's true!
The last leg of your journey,
Please see it through!

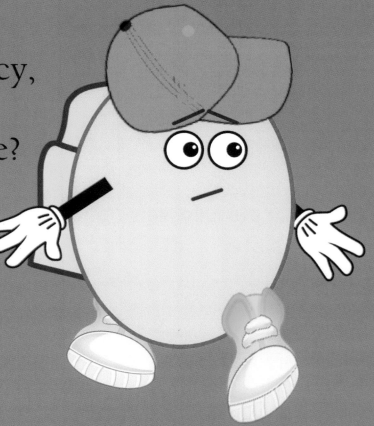

The beach? Puzzled Percy,
As he staggered away.
Why would she go there?
He just couldn't say.

The howling wind,
The crashing sea,
No place for a nut!
It's clear as can be!

Oh the Sea!
With the thought, Percy's heart jolted!
My poor sister,
She'll become ready salted!

He rushed to the coast
To rescue his sister!
But found when he got there...

...A most stunning vista!

An ocean so calm...

Palm trees and sand...

Nothing to fear...

Then just as she'd planned...

There was Pippa!

And with her, a coconut guy!

There on the beach
A nut like no other,
Big and bold
With hair all a flutter.

He crested the waves
On a surfboard no less!
Undoubtedly cool
(Though his hair *was* a mess).

The Nuts!

With thanks to publicdomainvectors.org
And Openclipart

Published by AMWT Books

Text and original illustrations © copyright 2020
by Alex M Wright
All rights reserved

The moral rights of Alex M Wright have been asserted